PERFECT THE PIG

by Susan Jeschke

Henry Holt and Company / New York

To my mother,
Victoria Kochman Newmark

Henry Holt and Company, Inc.
Publishers since 1866
115 West 18th Street
New York, New York 10011

Henry Holt is a registered trademark of Henry Holt and Company, Inc.

Published in Canada by Fitzhenry & Whiteside Ltd.,
195 Allstate Parkway, Markham, Ontario L3R 4T8.

Library of Congress Cataloging-in-Publication Data
Jeschke, Susan.   Perfect the pig.
Summary: A tiny pig is granted his wish which leads to an almost perfect life.
[1. Pigs—Fiction] I. Title.   PZ7.J553Pe   [E]   80-39998

ISBN 0-03-058622-4 (hardcover)
7   9   10   8
ISBN 0-8050-4704-2 (paperback)
3   5   7   9   10   8   6   4
First published in hardcover in 1980 by Holt, Rinehart and Winston
First Owlet paperback edition published in 1996 by Henry Holt and Company, Inc.
Printed in the United States of America on acid-free paper.∞

He was so small that his mother didn't know he was there. The other piglets were always pushing and shoving, squealing greedily for food, or rolling around in the mud.

But the tiny pig was gentle, quiet, and never greedy, and
he always kept clean.

While the other piglets played he would lie under his
favorite tree wishing for wings to carry him into the sky.

One day he heard a great shriek. A large sow had slip-
ped on the road. The little pig crawled under the fence
and ran to help her.

He wedged some pebbles and twigs under her, and with
great effort finally helped her to her feet.

The sow was very grateful and offered the little pig a wish—"anything at all," she said.

"I want wings," he answered.

The sow nodded and continued on her way. Almost at once wings began to grow on the little pig.

He was thrilled. His wings worked! He flew around all
day.

At night he returned to the pigpen. When the other pigs saw his wings they pushed him out. "Go sleep with the birds," they said.

He tried that, but the birds
wouldn't let him stay either.

On and on he flew towards a city.

He landed on a fire escape, too tired and hungry to go on. A woman came to the window. "So tiny, and with such beautiful wings. How perfect!" she said, lifting him inside.

She fed him, then put him to bed and kissed him
goodnight. The little pig kissed her back. This so
delighted the woman that she named the pig "Perfect."
Perfect could hardly believe it. He had not only found a
home, but someone who thought he was perfect.

Olive—that was the woman's name—was an artist. She adored Perfect and did all she could to please him. She bathed him . . .

. . . and fed him the choicest vegetables, some of which she grew in the apartment.

Soon she began to make pictures of Perfect posed among fruits and vegetables. He was a wonderful model.

However, he soon grew restless
and looked longingly at the sky.
Olive understood and took him up to the roof.

He flew about while she waited for him.

Olive made a little jacket to cover Perfect's wings so he wouldn't attract attention when she took him on walks.

But Perfect didn't like walking. The cement hurt his feet, and he couldn't see anything. So Olive carried him in her basket.

She tried her best to shelter him from the harsh things in life, but she didn't always succeed.

Whole Pigs
ALL SIZES

People liked the pictures of
Perfect and bought them.
Olive's savings jar began to fill up.

Soon the apartment was crowded with pictures, fruits and vegetables, and a growing Perfect. By now he had grown so much that he was getting too big to hide.

Olive decided that the best thing for both of them would be to live in the country. She pasted a label on her savings jar. It said HOUSE IN THE COUNTRY.

Perfect couldn't read, but he could see that Olive was very happy and excited. That made him happy and excited too.

But their happiness did not last long. The next day, while Perfect was out for his daily fly, a heavy fog rolled in. Perfect got lost. He flew around frantically as it grew darker and darker.

When the fog lifted, Perfect spotted a park bench. He landed on it and fell sound asleep. A man's gravelly voice woke him. "Well, I'll be—a pig with wings! My fortune is made!" the man said.

He picked Perfect up and ran home with him.

Perfect found himself in a small room. The man took off his belt and said, "okay, Oink. Now I'm going to train you. Fly around this room!" He cracked the belt, and Perfect flew away from it in fright. "That's a good Oink," the man said.

Then he emptied his garbage and gave it to Perfect to
eat. Perfect was shocked and ran to the window.

"Oh, no you don't," the man said, and tied Perfect to a pipe.

When the man was satisfied with the training he bought
Perfect a costume and took him to a park to perform.

At the end of the performance
Perfect would fly over the heads
of the audience.
Everyone oohed and ahhed
and the man collected lots of money.

Every night, after counting the money, the man gave Perfect a hard look and tied him up tighter. Once Perfect tried to resist and flapped his wings. "Trying to fly away, eh? I'll fix you, you flying porkchop," the man said.

He left the room and returned with a cage. From then on that was where Perfect was kept.

Perfect was miserable. His wings ached and he hadn't had a bath in months. The man gave him only garbage to eat and never ever kissed him. Every night Perfect cried himself to sleep thinking of Olive.

Olive went up to the roof each day and searched the sky for Perfect. She wandered through the streets looking for him.

Sometimes she wondered if Perfect had been a dream.
The one remaining picture of him reminded her that he
was real.

During one of her daily walks, she saw a sign that read
THE GREAT FLYING OINK. Olive immediately bought a
ticket and went in.

She could hardly believe her eyes. It was Perfect! The
man leaning over him was saying, "fly, you stupid
Oink—or it's off to the butcher with you!" But Perfect
couldn't budge. He was so sad, and his wings hurt.

"Perfect!" Olive cried out. Perfect raised his head. He
squealed as he stretched his wings and flew to her.
Everyone clapped.

Olive took off the leash. "Where are you going with my pig, lady?" the man said. "This is *my* pig," said Olive. The man and Olive began to argue. "Let a judge decide this," someone said. Everyone agreed.